Word List

Here is a list of words that might make it easier
to read this book. You'll find them in boldface
the first time they appear in the story.

| | |
|---|---|
| photographer | fuh-TOG-ruh-fer |
| turquoise | TER-koiz |
| adobe | uh-DOH-bee |
| pueblo | PWEB-loh |
| traditional | truh-DISH-uhn-ul |
| reservation | rez-ur-VAY-shun |
| elders | EL-derz |
| culture | KUL-cher |
| headdress | HED-dres |
| ceremony | SER-uh-moh-nee |
| galleries | GAL-er-eez |
| huevos rancheros | WUAY-vohs ran-CHAIR-ohs |
| symbols | SIM-bulz |
| mysterious | mis-TEAR-ee-us |
| coyotes | ky-OH-teez |
| Cerrillos | seh-REE-yos |
| Tijeras | tee-HER-ahz |

# Barbie™

# The Turquoise Trail Mystery

©1998 Mattel, Inc. Barbie and associated trademarks are owned and used under license from Mattel, Inc. All Rights Reserved. Published by Grolier Enterprises, Inc. Story by Rita Balducci and Judy Gitenstein. Photo crew: Willie Lew, Cristina LaBianca, James LaBianca, Greg Roccia, Rory Muir, and Judy Tsuno. Produced by Bumpy Slide Books. Printed in the United States of America.

ISBN: 0-7172-8799-8

Grolier Books

"Smile, Barbie!" called the **photographer**. Barbie smiled at the camera. It had been a long, hot day. But Barbie was a model. She was used to long photo shoots. Barbie was modeling jewelry for a catalog in Santa Fe, New Mexico. She stood in a large plaza in the center of the city. Some people walked along paths. Others sat on the grass and talked. Nearby, Native American artists were selling handmade crafts.

"Just one more necklace to shoot," the photographer said. He stood in the shade of a tree and put more film in the camera.

"I don't mind," Barbie replied. "This jewelry is beautiful."

Barbie carefully put on a silver and **turquoise** necklace. Then she smiled at the camera once again.

"Great!" the photographer said as he took another picture.

After a while, the photographer called, "That's a wrap!"

Barbie took off the necklace. She looked at it for a long time. The turquoise stone was the most beautiful blue-green color she had ever seen. She wanted to buy the necklace to remember her visit to Santa Fe. She hoped it was for sale.

Just then a smiling young woman with long, black hair came up to Barbie.

"Those pictures are going to be wonderful," the woman said. "I'm so glad the jewelry is going to be shown in the catalog."

Barbie smiled. "I was happy to get the job," she said. "I've always wanted to visit Santa Fe!"

"Oh, by the way, I'm Rosa," the woman said. "I made the necklace you were just wearing."

"How great!" Barbie said. "I was just going to ask if you knew who made it. It's my favorite piece, and I was hoping to buy it."

"Please, take it as a gift," Rosa said. "After all your hard work here, I'd like you to have it."

Barbie thanked Rosa. She loved her new gift. But Barbie was even happier to have met such a nice person.

"I'll walk you back to your hotel," Rosa said. "If you want, we can go the long way so you can see some of the city."

"I'd like that," Barbie said. "I want to learn as much as I can about Santa Fe while I'm here."

"Well, let's start right now," said Rosa. She pointed across the plaza. "That building is the Palace of the Governors. It was built in 1610. Now it's a museum."

They went to the covered walkway in front

of the building. Native American artists were busy selling jewelry, paintings, baskets, and clay pots. Barbie stopped to look at the crafts lined up in neat rows on colorful blankets.

Rosa went inside a candy store. She came back out with two pieces of candy. "Try this, Barbie. It's my favorite," she said. She handed Barbie a piece. Barbie thought the candy tasted wonderful, though it was a little spicy.

"What's in it?" Barbie asked.

"Nuts and sugar," Rosa replied. "Oh, and red chile peppers!"

"That explains it!" Barbie laughed.

Barbie and Rosa walked through the streets. Barbie admired the homes and buildings. Thick walls and flat roofs made them look like square boxes. And they came in more shades of brown than Barbie had ever seen.

Rosa ran her hand along a nearby wall.

"They're called **adobe** buildings," she said.

"They are made from mud and straw that baked in Santa Fe's hot sun. Some of them are hundreds of years old."

They stopped to look at an old church. "How lovely," said Barbie.

"It was built around 1636. That makes it one of the oldest churches in the country," Rosa said.

Rosa then pointed to a house across the street. "Over there," she began.

"Let me guess," Barbie said with a laugh, "is one of the oldest houses in Santa Fe."

"How did you know?" Rosa asked with a grin as they continued to walk.

"Tell me what it's like living here," Barbie said.

"Well, I live in a **pueblo** not far from Santa Fe. It's a real mix of past and present," Rosa told Barbie. "I'm a Pueblo Indian and was raised with **traditional** Indian beliefs. But I'm also a

businesswoman. I make and sell my jewelry all over the United States."

"Your jewelry is beautiful," Barbie told her.

"Thank you," replied Rosa. "I want to help keep Pueblo beliefs and traditions alive. The jewelry is a great way to do it."

"I hope this isn't a silly question," Barbie said shyly. "Is a pueblo the same thing as a **reservation**?"

"That's not a silly question at all," Rosa said. "I am a member of the Pueblo Indian nation. I live with my family on reservation land. The town we live in is called a pueblo. The word *pueblo* means 'village' in Spanish. But why don't you come see one for yourself? Take my business card, just in case you have time to visit me before you go back home."

"Thank you," Barbie said. She took Rosa's card.

"There's even a map on the back that shows

how to get to my house," said Rosa. "My pueblo isn't far from Santa Fe. Plus, it's a really pretty drive."

Barbie turned the card over. "This is the most beautiful map I've ever seen!" she cried. "It's more like a tiny work of art. I love the drawings of the houses and cactus plants."

"My sister, Susanna, drew that. She's an artist," Rosa said. Her face suddenly looked sad. "She used to love to make maps."

"What's wrong?" Barbie asked gently.

Rosa took a deep breath. "Let me start from the beginning," she said.

## Chapter Two

"My grandfather is one of the **elders** in our pueblo," Rosa began. "He's as close to a chief as we have."

Barbie listened closely. "Go on," she said.

"My grandfather and sister were very close," Rosa began. "But Susanna wanted to live in New York. She wanted to study different kinds of art. Grandfather didn't want her to go. He thought that if she moved away she'd forget her family and her Pueblo **culture**. They had a huge fight, and Susanna left. We haven't heard from her since."

"How awful," Barbie said. She and Rosa were now walking slowly through a park.

Rosa sighed. "It seems as if there's a black cloud over the whole pueblo," she said.

"What do you mean?" Barbie asked quietly.

"Well, a valuable **headdress** has disappeared. The mystery is, it was kept in a locked room. And Grandfather is the only one with the key."

"Did someone break in?" Barbie asked.

"No," Rosa said. "The room was fine. Nothing else was taken. It's as if the headdress just disappeared into thin air.

"That headdress has been worn in our pueblo's corn dance for many years," Rosa continued. "The dance is very important, because in it we ask for a large harvest. Now the elders won't allow any **ceremony** to take place until the headdress is found. I've even heard that some people think Grandfather had something to do with all this. But I just know he didn't. Grandfather

10

says that the black cloud will go away when Susanna comes back. I hope so, because I really miss her!"

"Oh, Rosa," Barbie said, "I'm so sorry."

"Thank you," said Rosa. "I wish Susanna knew how much we miss her. I know she'd come home right away."

They left the park and walked across the street to Barbie's hotel. Barbie thanked Rosa for the tour of the city and said good-bye. "I wish I could help Rosa find her sister," Barbie said to herself. "And the missing headdress, too."

Barbie woke up the next morning to the sound of the phone ringing.

"Good news!" said the photographer when Barbie answered. "The photos from yesterday's shoot look great! Why don't you take a few days off? We'll see you Monday morning."

"Terrific!" said Barbie. "See you then."

After she hung up, the phone rang again. It

was Rosa. "How would you like to continue your tour?" Rosa asked. "I got a postcard in the mail yesterday inviting me to an art show. It's at one of the best art **galleries** in Santa Fe. And the show's today. Can you come with me?"

Barbie leapt out of bed. "Yes, I'd love to!" she said.

"I'll pick you up in an hour!" said Rosa.

Barbie dressed in jeans, a white cotton shirt, and cowboy boots. Last, she put on her new necklace.

Barbie ate a tasty breakfast of cornbread, fresh fruit, and spicy fried eggs called *huevos rancheros*. She had just finished when Rosa knocked on the door. Rosa saw Barbie's necklace and smiled.

"Next stop, Canyon Road!" Rosa said. "Ready to go?"

"You bet!" Barbie declared.

Barbie grabbed her sunglasses and the two

new friends were off. After a short drive, Rosa and Barbie arrived at Canyon Road. Adobe buildings sat on both sides of the narrow street.

"This used to be an Indian trail," Rosa said. "But now most of these adobes are galleries that sell Native American art."

Barbie peeked in the door of each adobe they passed. She saw beautiful clay pots, paintings, and dolls carved from wood.

Rosa stopped in front of an adobe whose door was painted bright turquoise. "Here we are. This is the gallery on the postcard."

"What kind of art is being shown here?" Barbie asked.

"Many different kinds," said Rosa. "But the card didn't list any of the artists."

Barbie and Rosa went inside. Suddenly Rosa gasped.

In the middle of the room was a painting of an Indian chief. He was wearing a headdress with white and brown feathers. His face was old and wrinkled, but his eyes sparkled. Rosa walked toward the painting. Barbie followed her.

"Isn't that a wonderful painting?" a woman's voice asked from behind.

Surprised, Barbie turned around. The woman explained that she owned the gallery. Rosa still stared at the painting.

"Yes," Barbie said. "We like it very much. Can you tell us a little bit about it?"

"The man is wearing a Pueblo Indian headdress," the woman said. "I haven't seen one like it since I was a little girl."

"I have," whispered Rosa. Barbie and the owner turned to look at her. "That man is my grandfather," Rosa said.

Goose bumps rose up on Barbie's arms. Rosa turned to the owner.

"And I'm almost sure my sister is the artist," Rosa said firmly. "Are there any more paintings here by this artist?"

"Yes," the owner told Rosa. "This painting and two others arrived here about a week ago. They were tied up in brown paper. A note asked that I give the money from any sales to a Pueblo art school here in Santa Fe."

"Who signed the note?" Barbie asked.

"It wasn't signed. Neither are the paintings," the owner said. "There are only **symbols** where the artist's name usually is." She pointed to the bottom right-hand corner of the painting. There, Barbie saw a tiny drawing of a pair of scissors. The scissors looked like they were cutting through a blue line.

"Are the other two paintings still here?" Barbie asked.

"Yes," the owner said. She pointed to a

painting of a beautiful desert view at dusk. "This one's called *Red Desert*."

"Look! This one has a half-circle resting on a line in the corner of the painting," Barbie said.

The third painting was of a group of pine trees next to a dried-up stream. The owner said the painting was called *Morning View*. In the bottom right-hand corner was a squiggly line coming out of a box.

Rosa bought the painting of her grandfather. Barbie copied the other two symbols onto a piece of paper. Barbie and Rosa thanked the owner. Then they hurried to Rosa's car. "Now we have some clues," Barbie thought as she jumped in.

Barbie remembered Rosa's business card with the small map and symbols on the back.

"Barbie, are you thinking what I'm thinking?" Rosa asked.

"Yes! Those symbols remind me of the ones Susanna uses in her maps," Barbie replied. "But how can we figure out what the three symbols mean?"

"All of Susanna's maps are at my house," Rosa said. "Maybe they can give us some clues to what these symbols mean. Will you help me?"

"Sure," said Barbie. "Let's stop at the hotel so I can pack a bag."

"Great!" said Rosa. "Let's go!"

Chapter Three

The friends rode away from Santa Fe to
Rosa's pueblo. They drove farther into the desert.
Barbie saw fewer houses and more green and
yellow cactus plants.

"Wow!" Barbie said aloud. "If I were an
artist, I'd want to live here, too. The whole place
looks like one big postcard!"

All Barbie could see for miles was desert
and large mountains in the distance. "I'm glad
you've got a full tank of gas," Barbie said to
Rosa. "I wouldn't want to get stuck out here."

They passed a road sign for Rosa's pueblo.

18

A few miles later, Rosa made the turnoff. She drove down a dirt road and soon came to a small town. Rosa parked her car near a building that looked like a school.

"I'm so glad you're here," Rosa said as she and Barbie got out of the car. "Last night, I told my family all about the photo shoot. Everyone wants to meet you!"

Rosa carried the painting as they walked down the main street. Some kids were playing nearby. Barbie saw adobe houses just like the ones she had seen in Santa Fe. But here, some of the older houses had ladders leading up to the second story.

"It's beautiful here," Barbie said. "We should have had the photo shoot right here in your pueblo."

"Many pueblos don't allow people to take pictures," Rosa said. "We love visitors. But we ask that you put the memories in your head, not

your camera!"

The two friends walked on as Rosa told Barbie about the pueblo.

"Although these houses are old, most of them have modern things inside, like microwaves and dishwashers. One of the pueblos near here even has a golf course," Rosa said. "But some of the elders don't have or even want telephones."

"Wow!" Barbie said. "The mix of old and new sounds just right!"

Rosa stopped at one of the houses. "This is the tribal leader's office," Rosa said as they entered the building. A man was seated behind a shiny wooden desk with a computer on it. When Barbie and Rosa came in, he put down the telephone and stood up.

"Dad, I'd like you to meet Barbie," Rosa said. "Barbie, meet my father, Daniel Youngdeer. He is the leader of this pueblo," she said proudly.

"Welcome, Barbie!" Rosa's father said as he shook her hand. "We're all happy that our crafts will be shown in the catalog. It will also help bring visitors to the Pueblo Arts and Crafts Show we have every year. We carry the old ways inside our hearts. Sharing our art helps us show our ways to others."

"I'm so happy to be a part of it," Barbie said.

"Dad, Barbie and I have something to share with you," Rosa said.

Rosa handed her father the wrapped painting. Barbie and Rosa watched as he pulled away the paper. He was so surprised that he took a step back.

"It's Father!" he said. "Where did you find it?"

Rosa and Barbie told him about the gallery and the three **mysterious** paintings.

"I knew it was Grandfather the minute I saw this painting," Rosa began. "The gallery owner doesn't know who painted it. But I know it was Susanna."

"And look here," Barbie said, pointing to

the symbol at the bottom corner of the painting. "The other two paintings had symbols, too."

"And you know how much Susanna likes drawing symbols on her maps," Rosa added.

"Well, this is great news! It's the first clue we've had about Susanna since she left," Mr. Youngdeer said.

"Susanna's maps might help us learn what the symbols on the paintings mean," Rosa said to her father. "Barbie, let's go to my house and take a look."

"I'll go with you," Rosa's father said.

Rosa gave her father a quick kiss. "It's okay, Dad. I know you want to find Susanna, too. But you've got important work to do. Why don't you let us see what we can find out? We'll give you a full report at dinner. I promise!"

"Thanks, honey," her father said. "See you in a few hours."

## Chapter Four

When the two friends reached Rosa's house, Rosa hurried inside. She rushed over to a desk in the corner of the room and opened one of the drawers. Then she took out a large map and set it on the dining room table.

Barbie used her finger to trace the roads from Santa Fe. "The symbols really do look like the ones on the painting," she said. "This one most of all."

Barbie put her finger on a curving turquoise-colored line. "It's something called the Turquoise Trail," she read aloud.

Rosa looked closely. "Barbie, that's it!" she said. "I'll bet Susanna drew the blue line on her painting to symbolize where she is. She's somewhere on the Turquoise Trail!"

"What's the Turquoise Trail?" asked Barbie.

"It's a two-lane road outside of Santa Fe that heads south," Rosa said. "There are a few houses along the way. But mostly it's just jackrabbits and snakes for forty-six miles. In the last few years, artists have moved along the trail to paint where it's quiet. It's a perfect place to hide out."

"I'll bet that's where Susanna did the painting of your grandfather," Barbie said. "I've got two days off. Why don't we go right now?"

"It's too late to start out today," Rosa said. "We'll stay the night here at the pueblo. Then we'll start first thing in the morning."

Rosa and Barbie decided to take a walk before dinner. As they walked, Barbie saw horses grazing in a nearby field. A beautiful palomino trotted over to the fence where they were standing. It nuzzled Barbie's hand.

"Would you like to ride him?" Rosa asked.

"I'd love to," Barbie said. Rosa helped Barbie saddle up the horse.

Barbie and Rosa got on their horses. Then Rosa called out to Barbie, "Come on! Let's follow the path that circles the pueblo."

Barbie gently tapped the horse's side and yelled, "Giddyyap!" And off they went.

Barbie leaned back in the saddle and watched the sunset. The sky was filled with as many colors as an artist's paint box.

Rosa and her horse trotted up to Barbie. "I can't wait to go to the Turquoise Trail tomorrow," said Rosa.

"I know," said Barbie. "It's going to be hard to sleep tonight!"

"Well, a good dinner will help," Rosa said.

"My mom's a great cook." Then she tapped her horse on the side with her heels. Rosa led Barbie around the rest of the trail.

When Rosa and Barbie returned from their ride, dinner was ready.

"Grandfather is not feeling well enough to join us," said Mrs. Youngdeer to Rosa as they sat down to eat.

"Don't worry, Mom," Rosa said softly. "Perhaps he'll feel better tomorrow. And maybe Barbie and I will bring back good news."

"Everything is so tasty, Mrs. Youngdeer," said Barbie. She had just finished her second bowl of roasted corn soup. "I didn't realize how hungry I was."

"Try the salad," Rosa's mother said.

"Umm, it's wonderful," Barbie said. "I never knew green beans could taste so good."

Rosa and her parents smiled at each other.

"That's cactus," Rosa said.

"Cactus?" Barbie asked. She quickly took a sip of her fruit punch.

Rosa's mother laughed. "Don't worry," she said. "We took out all the prickly parts."

"Whew!" Barbie said with a laugh.

The talk soon turned to Barbie and Rosa's plans for the next day.

"Do you really think Susanna could be on the Turquoise Trail?" Rosa's mother asked hopefully.

"I think there's a pretty good chance," Rosa said.

"Then I should go with you," her mother said.

"Mom," Rosa said gently, "I know you miss Susanna and want her home. But what if we're wrong and she's not there? I don't want you to go on a wild-goose chase. If we do find Susanna, I promise we'll try to get her to come home with us."

"There are just a few old ghost towns along the way. You won't be able to get help if you run into trouble," her mother said.

Rosa giggled. "Now you're being silly!" she said. "You know that tourists drive the Trail all the time. Besides, Barbie and I will be together the whole time."

Rosa's father spoke up. "If Susanna painted those pictures, then there's a chance that she wanted someone to find them." Then he gave his cellular phone to Rosa. "And don't worry, dear," he said to his wife. "The girls can use this to call us if they need to."

After dinner, Barbie and Rosa each took a cup of Mexican hot chocolate out to the back porch. Barbie breathed in deeply to smell the chocolate and cinnamon smells.

"No matter how old I get, my mom still thinks of me as her baby," said Rosa.

"I know what you mean," Barbie told her. "I guess families are the same all over. Moms and Dads always worry about their children, even when they're not children anymore!"

"I guess that's true," Rosa said. They sat and watched the stars. They could hear the long howls of **coyotes** in the distance.

Finally Rosa stood up and yawned. "We have a big day tomorrow," she said to Barbie. "Let's get some sleep. I'll show you where the guest room is."

Later, as Barbie snuggled under her blanket, she thought about tomorrow's journey. It seemed even more exciting because they had a mystery to solve. "I sure hope we'll be able to find Susanna," she thought, "and that she'll want to come home."

With the cool wind coming through the window, Barbie quickly fell asleep. She dreamed of riding across the desert on a beautiful horse.

Chapter Five

The next morning, Barbie and Rosa were up with the sun. They wanted to get an early start. After breakfast, Rosa's mother packed them a picnic lunch and many bottles of water.

Rosa's father gave them a photograph of Susanna. "Show this picture to people. Perhaps someone will know her," he explained.

"Or have an idea where she might be," Rosa's mother added.

Rosa kissed her parents good-bye. Then she and Barbie got in the car.

"Good luck!" Rosa's parents called to them.

Barbie and Rosa waved as they pulled away from the house.

"It would make my parents so happy to see Susanna again," Rosa said.

"Let's keep our fingers crossed," Barbie replied. "And maybe they'll get their wish!"

The Turquoise Trail was a quiet road with cactus plants and wildflowers growing on both sides.

"There sure isn't much traffic," Barbie said.

"This is a very old road," Rosa explained as she drove. "If people are in a hurry, they take the new interstate. The Turquoise Trail is for people who want to drive slowly and enjoy the beautiful views."

Barbie and Rosa soon came to a sleepy town called **Cerrillos**. Clouds of dust rose in the air when Rosa parked the car. "Gosh," Barbie said, "I feel like I'm in a western movie. Where is everybody?"

Rosa explained, "During the Gold Rush of the 1890s, this town was filled with miners. They thought they'd dig up enough gold, silver, and turquoise to get rich. When they left years ago, the hotels, saloons, and shops shut down. Now only a few stores are open for business. The rest is a ghost town."

"Oh, my!" said Barbie. "Of course, there's no such thing as ghosts, right?" She and Rosa both looked worried, but then they burst into laughter.

They spotted a man opening up a gas station. They showed him Susanna's picture and asked if he had seen her. The man hadn't. Barbie and Rosa looked and looked but couldn't find another person in the town.

"Let's get going. This place is a little spooky," Rosa said.

"Good idea," Barbie said. "There's no one else here to ask if they've seen Susanna, anyway. Except maybe for some ghosts," she added with a

giggle as they got in the car.

They headed south. Before long Barbie and Rosa arrived at the town of Madrid.

"For a ghost town, this is a pretty busy place," Barbie said. They drove slowly down the main street. It was full of tourists.

"This is the only really busy town along the Turquoise Trail," Rosa said. "That means it probably has a big general store. If Susanna is living anywhere along this trail, she'd have to buy her food there."

Barbie and Rosa went straight to the town's general store. Rosa took out the photo of Susanna. She showed it to the man standing behind the counter. "Yup, I've seen her," he said. "Comes in once a week or so to buy food. Art stuff, too. But I don't know where she lives."

Barbie and Rosa thanked him. Then they sat down at the counter and had ice cream sodas to celebrate their new clue.

When they were done, Barbie and Rosa jumped back in the car. As she drove, Rosa thought out loud. "We know Susanna's somewhere along this trail. But where? If we don't figure out what the three symbols mean, we'll never find her."

Barbie touched her friend's arm. "Don't worry, Rosa. We'll figure it out," Barbie said. "A good detective always follows her hunches. And yours have been right so far."

After a while, Barbie saw more old buildings and an adobe church coming into view. "The map says this next town is called Golden," Barbie said.

"It used to be a gold-mining town," Rosa told her. "That's how it got its name."

Barbie looked down at her watch. "Oh, my goodness!" she said. "It's already one o'clock! Time sure flies when you're looking for clues."

"Let's stop and eat the lunch my mom

packed for us," Rosa said.

"Good idea," said Barbie. Rosa drove to a picnic area at a place called Rattlesnake Springs. They took their picnic basket to a table beside the road.

"I think I can guess how this place got its name, too," Barbie said, looking around. She took a bite of the taco that Rosa's mother had made. "I just hope there are no rattlesnakes around."

"Maybe just a few," said Rosa with a laugh. "Don't worry. They won't bother you if you don't bother them."

But as Barbie ate her lunch, she couldn't help thinking about snakes hiding in the bushes. She was happy when they got back in the car and started driving again.

"Let's keep our fingers crossed," Rosa said.

"And think good thoughts," added Barbie.

They had been driving for a while when

they came to a fork in the road. "**Tijeras** Canyon is up ahead," said Rosa, reading the road sign. "I think we're getting close to the end of the Turquoise Trail."

Barbie looked carefully at the map as Rosa drove. "Hmm," Barbie said aloud. "Do you know any Spanish, Rosa? Because, if my hunch is right—"

"*Tijeras* means 'scissors' in Spanish!" Rosa shouted. "Just like the scissors in the painting!"

"The first symbol must mean that Susanna is living in Tijeras Canyon!" Barbie added.

Chapter Six

Rosa turned off the Turquoise Trail onto a
dirt road. As she headed toward Tijeras Canyon,
Barbie studied the second symbol. Soon they
came upon an area with houses. Rosa parked the
car and took Susanna's photo out of her bag.

"This is a good place to show people
Susanna's picture," Rosa said. She had opened her
car door when Barbie grabbed her arm.

"Wait a minute, Rosa!" Barbie said. "I think
there's a faster way. Look at this."

Barbie showed her the second symbol, a
half-circle resting on a line. Then she gave Rosa

the map. Barbie pointed to a road off Tijeras Canyon.

Rosa studied the map for a moment. Then her face lit up.

"Sunset Road!" Rosa said. "It's a symbol for a sunset! That has to be it! Let's go!"

Rosa followed the map to Sunset Road.

"We're on the right track," Barbie stated. "The scissors symbol led us to Tijeras Canyon and the setting sun led us to Sunset Road."

"But what does the symbol on the *Morning View* painting mean?" Rosa asked.

Suddenly they saw a group of pine trees next to a dried-up stream.

"It's the same view as from the painting!" Barbie exclaimed.

Rosa stopped the car at the trees. Then the two friends saw a curvy driveway that led to a tiny cabin. They looked at each other, then at the symbol written on the notepad.

They realized that the squiggly line coming out of the box looked like the driveway. The curved line in the box looked like an S.

"The *S* stands for *Susanna!*" Barbie and Rosa shouted together. The two friends raced to the house. Barbie and Rosa stepped onto the porch. Rosa knocked on the cabin door, waited a minute, then knocked again.

"No one's home," Rosa said finally. As she turned and stepped off the porch, the front door opened.

Barbie found herself face-to-face with a dark-haired woman. She seemed to be just a few years older than Barbie.

"May I help you?" the woman asked. She held a paintbrush in one hand. Then she spotted Rosa.

"Rosa?" the woman asked.

Rosa turned around. With a huge smile on her face, she leapt onto the porch and hugged her sister.

"Susanna!" Rosa cried. "I'm so happy to see

you! This is my friend Barbie. She helped me find you. Barbie, this is my sister, Susanna."

Susanna and Barbie smiled and shook hands. Susanna showed them to a bench on the porch. "Please sit down," she said.

The two sisters were quiet for a moment. Neither knew where to begin.

"The painting of your grandfather is beautiful," Barbie told Susanna. "I can tell you care for him very much."

Susanna blinked, her black eyes filling with tears. "I do," she replied. "Since I've been here, I've realized something very important. Being a Pueblo Indian is something I take with me wherever I go. I carry it with me in my heart."

"That's exactly what Dad says!" Rosa exclaimed. "We followed the clues you left on the paintings to find you."

Susanna smiled shyly. "I was hoping that would work," she said. "I sent you the postcard about the art show. I thought you'd figure out the clues once you saw my paintings in the gallery. I drew the symbols to let you know I was okay. And where I was."

"But why?" asked Rosa. "Why didn't you just come home?"

"When I left home," Susanna began, "I was so angry at Grandfather, I didn't want to talk to anyone. I went to New York to attend art school. But I wasn't really happy. I realized I missed everyone very much. So I decided to come home."

"Then why are you here?" Barbie asked.

"Painting a person's picture is a way of showing your love," Susanna said. "I came here first to paint a picture of Grandfather. I was going to give it to him as a way of saying 'I'm sorry.' But then something awful happened."

"What?" Rosa asked with a worried look.

"You know I've always loved the headdress from the corn dance. I wanted to paint Grandfather wearing it," Susanna said. "I drove to the village one night just to borrow it. I had a copy of the key to the room where it's kept. Nobody knew about it. I was using the headdress as a model. But then I spilled yellow paint on it. I tried to clean the feathers, but I just made it worse."

Susanna sniffed. "Now I'm afraid to go back. Everyone will be upset with me for ruining the headdress. Especially Grandfather."

"Susanna, we've been so worried about you," Rosa said softly. "And Grandfather cares more about you than he does about the headdress. Please come home. We miss you. *Grandfather* misses you."

"Really?" asked Susanna.

Susanna smiled and hugged her sister. "Thank you, Rosa," she said.

"I just wish we'd found you sooner," said Rosa.

"But," Barbie added, "it's been fun looking for you!" All three women laughed.

Susanna stood up. "Come inside. I'll show you the headdress," she said.

Barbie and Rosa followed her into the house. It was a cozy-looking place. A cat slept on a rocking chair. In the corner were paints and a canvas. Susanna went over to an old trunk. She opened it up and lifted out the headdress.

"It's beautiful," Barbie said.

Rosa gently touched the feathers. "The paint spot isn't so bad," she said. "I'm sure it can be fixed."

"You know," Rosa continued, "Dad and Grandfather have been talking. Grandfather understands that the best way to keep the old ways alive is to share them with others. Dad told him that there are many ways to keep our traditions alive. One way is through your painting."

"So you don't think he'll be angry with me?" Susanna asked.

"I think he will understand," said Rosa.

"Just give me a few minutes to pack a bag," said Susanna, "and then I'll be ready to go."

Rosa drove back along the Turquoise Trail the way they had come. But this time they didn't stop at any of the towns. Susanna was nervous, but excited, too. She couldn't wait to see her family again.

The pueblo was quiet when they returned. "Everyone must be inside having dinner," Rosa said. She stopped the car in front of her family's house.

"I've thought about home every day since I left," Susanna said. She stepped out of the car. "Being away has made me see just how important my family is to me."

"I know what you mean," said Barbie. She couldn't wait to get home and tell her sisters about her adventure.

Susanna, Barbie, and Rosa stopped at the front door. Susanna knocked, as if she were a guest. Then the door opened. Susanna stood face-to-face with her father.

"Susanna!" he said as he wrapped his arms around his daughter.

Rosa and Barbie followed them into the living room. Rosa's mother ran in to give Susanna a hug, too. With all the hugging and shouting, no one saw the elderly man who was standing in the shadows.

"My child," he said with tears in his eyes.

"Grandfather," Susanna said in a quiet voice.

Barbie and Rosa smiled as grandfather and granddaughter put their arms around each other.

"Grandfather, I have something to return to our people," Susanna said. "And something to tell you." She went to her bag and pulled out the headdress. "I'm sorry I damaged it."

He looked at the headdress. Then he smiled. "Any mistakes are part of our past. You are part of our future. Nothing is as important as your being home."

The next day, Rosa and Susanna's family gave a huge party. Everyone in the pueblo was invited. Barbie looked at the happy faces of the people in the pueblo. But none looked happier than Susanna's.

That evening, there was a traditional storytelling circle around a fire. Barbie listened as each person, young and old, told a story.

All at once, Barbie missed her sisters. "I have so many stories to tell them," she thought with a happy sigh.

The old chief sat with a blanket around his shoulders. He held his granddaughter's hand tightly. They both smiled at Barbie.

Barbie looked around at Susanna and Rosa and their family. "This is a moment I'll never forget," Barbie thought. She felt so lucky to share in their happiness.

Rosa went over and whispered something

in Susanna's ear. Then Susanna got up. She and Rosa came and sat beside Barbie. From behind her back, Rosa brought out a thin loop of leather. It had a shiny black feather tied to it. She placed it around Barbie's neck.

"This feather is our gift to you because you helped bring our family back together," Rosa explained. "Thank you."

"From all of us," added Susanna.

"I'm glad I could help," Barbie said. "Thank you for making me feel so welcome! This feather will always be special to me. I will treasure it forever." She gave Rosa and Susanna each a hug.

"Then be careful," said Susanna with a wink. "I hear that things with feathers have a way of disappearing!"